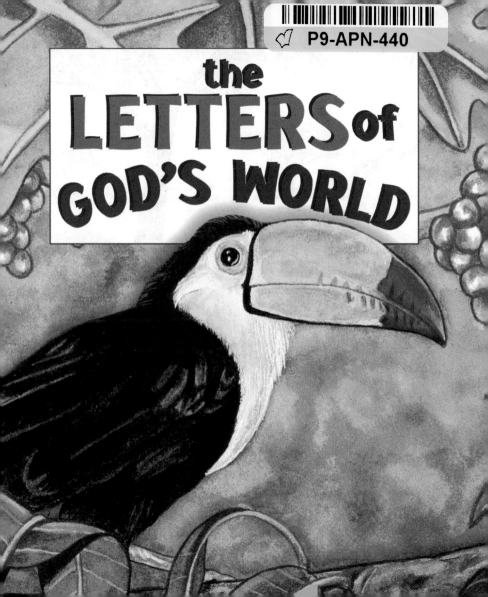

the LETTERS of GOD'S WORLD

A God made an **a**ntelope and an **a**cacia tree that live on the grassy plains of Africa.

B God made a **b**umblebee that flies among wildflowers called **b**uttercups, and a **b**adger that lives in a **b**urrow.

C God made a **c**oyote that lives among the prickly **c**actus in a **c**anyon in the desert.

D God made a **d**unlin, a shorebird that lives by the **d**unes of the seashore.

E God made an **egret**, a wading bird that hunts for fish among the sawgrass in the **e**verglades of Florida.

F God made a frog that sits on a fallen tree and the leafy green ferns in a shady forest.

G God made a ground squirrel that stands surrounded by the tall grasses and yellow wildflowers, called goldenrod, in the grasslands of North America.

H

God made **honeybees** that buzz around the flowers of a **hawthorn** tree in a **hedgerow** of Europe.

I God made an iguana, a lizard that lives inland on the islands of the Galapagos.

J God made a jaguar that rests on the limb
of a jacaranda tree in the jungles of
South America.

K God made a **k**angaroo that jumps across the dry floodplains of the **K**akadu region in Australia.

L God made a loon, a bird that carries its baby on its back as it swims across the water of a lake where it lives.

M God made a marmot and the bright green moss that live on the rocks high in the mountains of Western America.

N God made the **n**ewt that stands on a log and the **n**eedles on an evergreen tree that live in the **n**orthwest woods of America.

O God made an **o**tter that wraps itself in kelp as it floats **o**ffshore in the **o**cean by the coast of California.

P God made **p**uffins, colorful birds that live on the rocky cliffs near the **P**acific ocean in Alaska.

Q God made a **q**uail, a game-bird that lives among pretty white wild-flowers, called **Q**ueen Anne's Lace, in a **q**uiet ravine.

R God made a raccoon and a cluster of tall stemmed grasses, called reeds, that live on the banks of a river.

S God made sponges that look like tall purple tubes and the bright pink sunstar that live under the ocean waves by the seashore.

T God made a toucan, a bird with a large colorful beak that perches on the branch of a tree in the tropical rain-forest of South America.

U

God made an **u**rchin with brigh[t] purple spines and a **u**nivalve seashel[l] that live **u**nderwater on a coral reef.

V

God made a **v**ole, a small rodent that lives in the grassy undergrowth of a mountain **v**alley.

W God made a weasel and the bright yellow waxy cap mushrooms that live in the woods of North America.

X God made a fox that sits among the blue wild-flowers, called flax, in the fields of Texas.

Y God made yellowjackets that hover by the flowers of the yarrow plant in a national park called Yosemite.